KT-529-171

The Drop Goes Plop

A first look at the water cycle

368009

ok is to l
dat

For all the raindrops at Burgess Hill School – SG
Thanks for everything John and Pamela – SA

First published in Great Britain in 1998 by Macdonald Young Books,
an imprint of Wayland Publishers Ltd
61 Western Road
Hove
East Sussex
BN3 1JD

Find Macdonald Young Books on the internet at
http://www.myb.co.uk

Concept and design by Liz Black
Commissioning Editor Dereen Taylor
Language Consultant Ann Lazim, Centre for Language in Primary Education
Science Consultant Dr Carol Ballard

Text © Sam Godwin
Illustrations © Simone Abel
Book © Macdonald Young Books
M.Y.Bees © Clare Mackie

A CIP catalogue record for this book
is available from the British Library

ISBN 07500 2495 X

Printed and bound in Asa, Portugal

The Drop Goes Plop

A first look at the water cycle

FALKIRK COUNCIL

MACDONALD YOUNG BOOKS

A cloud forms high up in the sky. It grows bigger

and bigger and bigger...
Mama, what is a cloud?
A cloud is millions of drops of water. The sun's heat sucks them out of the sea.

A strong wind blows the cloud
There are all sorts of clouds. There are ice clouds, thunder clouds and rain clouds, like this one.
I thought so! I can see the drops of water. Let's follow that really big drop.

over hills and fields and little towns.

Raindrops fall from the cloud. The big drop
I'm singing in the rain...
When the cloud gets heavy, the drops fall out as rain. If it's really cold, the drops freeze and fall as snow or hail.

goes plop. It runs down the baby gull's feathers.

Down, down, down falls the drop

until – splash! – it lands in a flowing river.

The drop is carried along the river – past houses

and under bridges.

At last the drop floats into a peaceful reservoir.
A reservoir is a lake with a dam at one end. Water is stored here until people need it.

Then, a dam is opened...

Poor drop! It is sucked into a cleaning station

and pushed up a pipe into a water tower. Where is it going now?

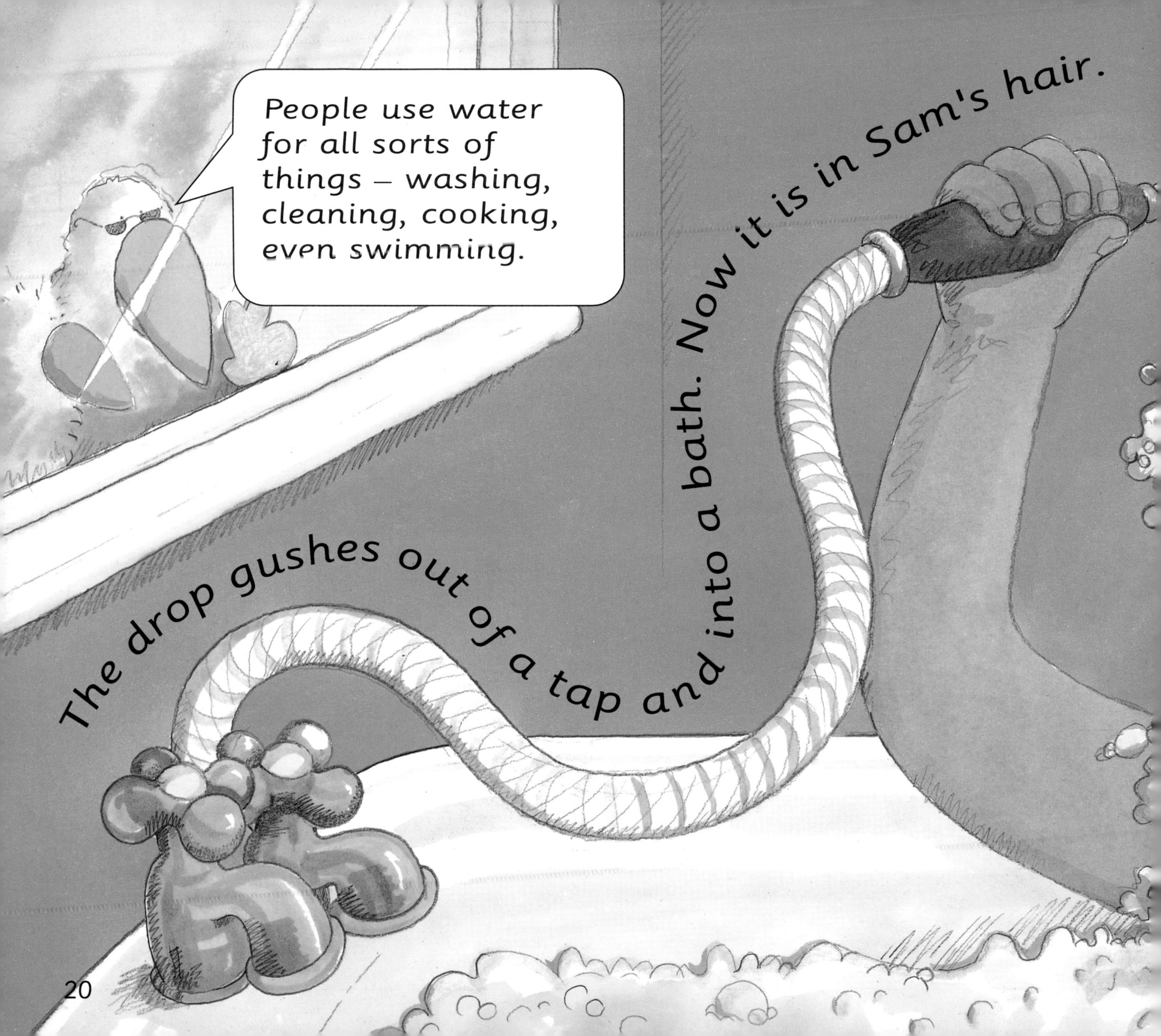
People use water for all sorts of things – washing, cleaning, cooking, even swimming.
The drop gushes out of a tap and into a bath. Now it is in Sam's hair.

The shampoo bubbles foam and splutter!

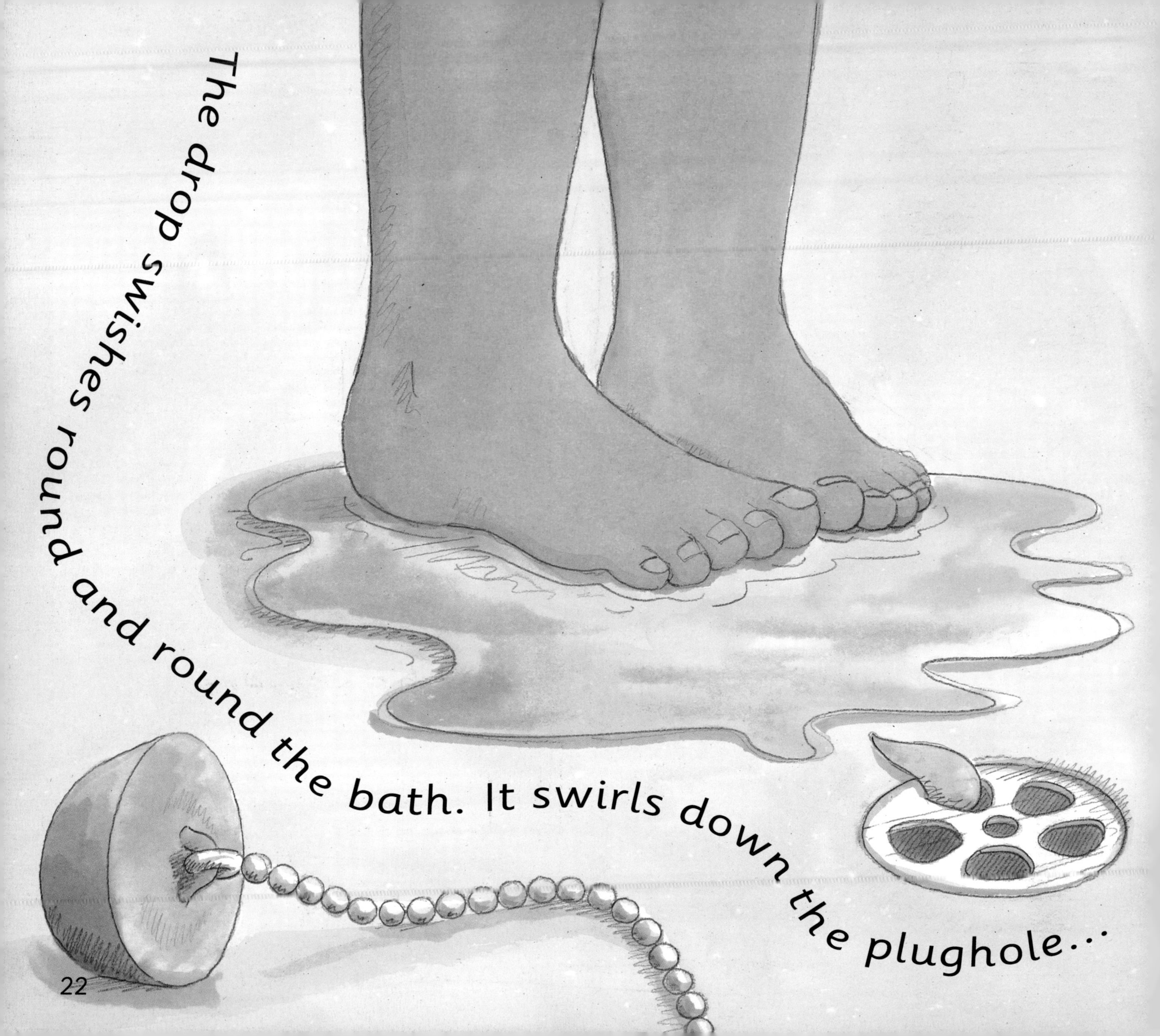

The drop swishes round and round the bath. It swirls down the plughole...

Poor drop. It whooshes down a pipe into the sewers.

At the sewage works the drop travels through tanks and filters. Soon it is squeaky clean again.

Water gets dirty after it has been used and has to be cleaned again.
It passes through a pipe that leads to...

...THE SEA. The drop rises up into the air again.

It joins millions of other drops in a cloud.
Mama, will we ever see my special drop again?
Maybe. Water moves in a never-ending cycle.

Then the drop goes plop.

Its amazing journey starts all over again.

Useful Words

Cleaning station
A place where water from rivers and reservoirs is cleaned for people to use at home.

Dam
An enormous wall built to keep water in a reservoir.

Filter
A container of sand and gravel that is used to clean water. As water passes through the filter, dirt sticks to the sand and gravel.

Reservoir
A huge lake that has been specially made to store water.

River
A large stream of water. Rivers start as small streams on top of hills or mountains. As a river flows it gets wider and deeper. It eventually flows into the sea.

Sewer
An underground system of drains and pipes that carries used water from our homes. The dirty water passes to a sewage works where it is cleaned before it is pumped into the sea.

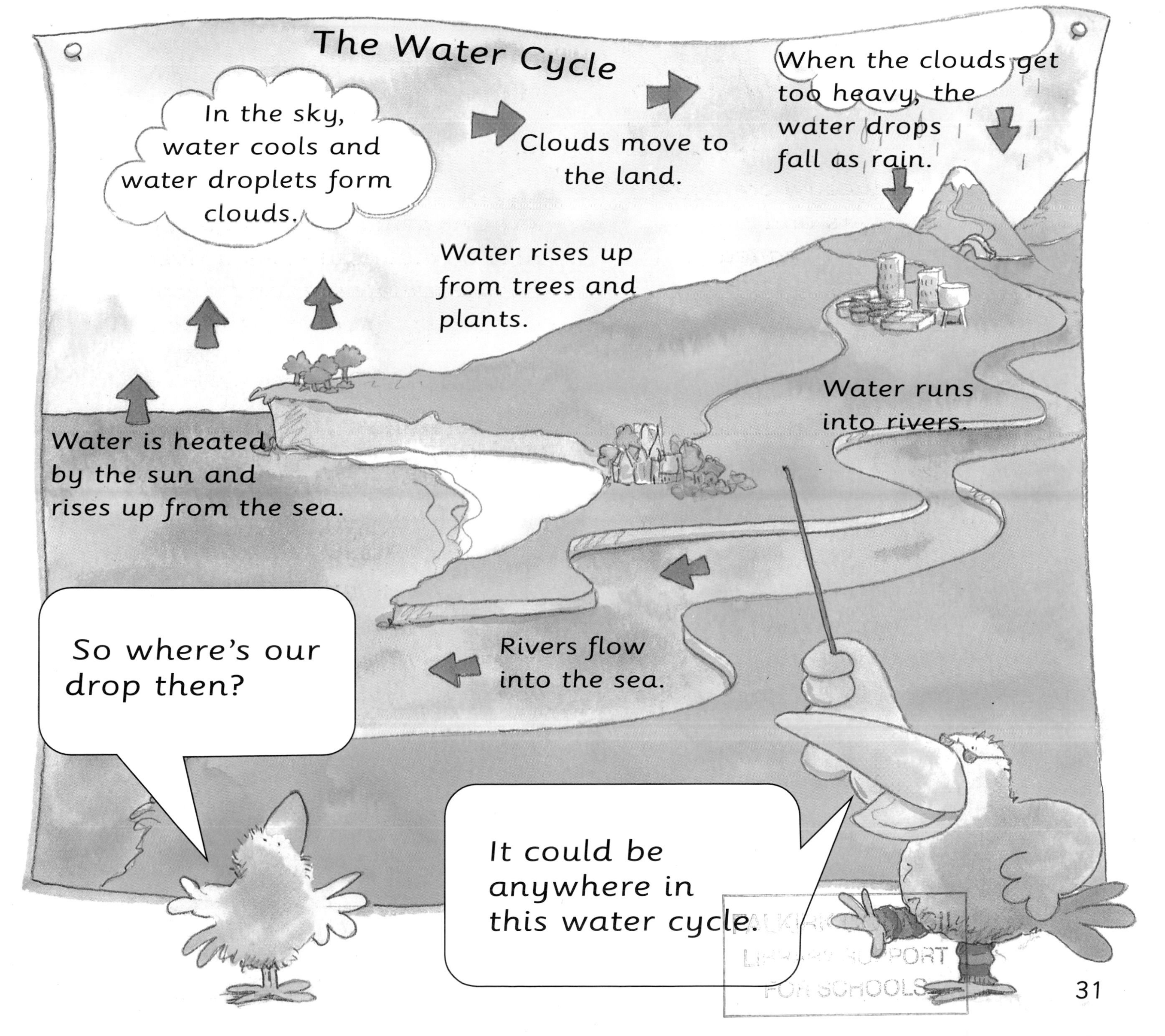

FALKIRK COUNCIL LIBRARY SUPPORT FOR SCHOOLS